Dear Parents:

Children learn to read in stages, and all children develop reading skills at different ages. **Ready Readers**™ were created to promote children's interest in reading and to increase their reading skills. **Ready Readers**™ are written on two levels to accommodate children ranging in age from three through eight. These stages are meant to be used only as a guide.

Stage 1: Preschool-Grade 1
Stage 1 books are written in very short, simple sentences with large type. They are perfect for children who are getting ready to read or are just becoming familiar with reading on their own.

Stage 2: Grades 1-3
Stage 2 books have longer sentences and are a bit more complex. They are suitable for children who are able to read but still may need help.

All the **Ready Readers**™ tell varied, easy-to-follow stories and are colorfully illustrated. Reading will be fun, and soon your child will not only be ready, but eager to read.

Lost At Sea

Written by Frances P. Max
Illustrated by Frank and Carol Hill

Modern Publishing
A Division of Unisystems, Inc.
New York, New York 10022

Wanda Whale loved to read about far away places.

"I want to meet new people," she told her mother, "I want to see new places."

"I'm sure that we can find many new things for you to see," Wanda's mother said, "Let's go for a swim with your father."

Wanda swam behind her parents.
They dove deep into the sea.

First they saw Fred Fish. He was
selling junk.

"Do you want to buy anything?" he asked the Whale family.

"No thank you," Wanda said as she and her parents swam away.

Next, Wanda met Opal Octopus.
"I'm riding my tricycle to dance
class. Do you want to meet my
teacher, Madame Lobster?"
Opal asked.

"No thank you," Wanda
said, "I have more new
things to see and do."

Nearby, Chris Crab played with a mermaid in the sand. "I am building a sand castle," he said, "Do you want to help?"

"No thank you," Wanda said.

Wanda swam toward beautiful, pink coral. But, when she turned around, she couldn't find her parents. "Oh no!" Wanda cried, "They must not have seen me swim away."

Wanda looked left. But she only saw fish and seaweed. She looked right. But all she saw was an old boat.

Wanda swam to the shore. But
her parents were not there either.
She started to cry.

"I can't find my mom and dad,"
Wanda told her friends.

Gulliver Gull told Wanda to talk
to Sam Clam.

"He can find anything,"
Gulliver said.

So Wanda swam back down to
the bottom of the sea.

Sam Clam was very busy.
There were many fish waiting to
talk to him.

Wanda didn't want to wait.
She wanted to find her parents now!

Wanda was still crying when Gulliver flew by and landed on her back.

"Maybe I can help you with my binoculars," he said.

Then Gulliver jumped up and down. "I see them!" he shouted, "Just keep swimming!"

Wanda was so happy to see her parents that she swam as fast as she could to meet them.

Wanda's father thanked Gulliver for his help. "It has been a long day. We have seen enough new people and new places for one day. Let's swim home," he said.

Wanda's parents kept an eye on her all the way home.